MAEVE BINCHY
THE BUILDERS

Maeve Binchy was born in Dublin in 1940. After
a spell as a schoolteacher, she worked as an *Irish
Times* journalist for many years. She began to
write fiction while in her early forties, and wrote
fourteen novels which became bestsellers in over
thirty languages. Her stories have been adapted
for stage, television and cinema. She lives in
Dalkey with her husband, writer Gordon Snell.

GEMMA

Open Door

THE BUILDERS
First published by GemmaMedia in 2009.

GemmaMedia
230 Commercial Street
Boston MA 02109 USA
617 938 9833
www.gemmamedia.com

Printed in the United States of America
Cover design by Artmark

14   13   9 10 11

ISBN: 978-1-934848-16-6

        Library of Congress Cataloging-in-Publication Data

Binchy, Maeve.
  The builders / Maeve Binchy.
        p. cm.
  ISBN 978-1-934848-16-6   (pbk.)
  1.   Middle-aged women--Fiction. 2.   Contractors--Fiction. 3.   Family secrets--Fiction.
Title.
  PR6052.I7728B85   2011
  823'.914--dc22

                                        2011019350

OPEN DOOR SERIES

An innovative program of original
works by some of our most
beloved modern writers and
important new voices. First designed
to enhance adult literacy in Ireland,
these books affirm the truth that
a story doesn't have
to be big to open the world.

Patricia Scanlan
Series Editor

OPEN DOOR

For Gordon
with all my love

Chapter One

Nan at Number Fourteen Chestnut Road heard about the builders from Mr O'Brien, the fussy man at Number Twenty-eight.

'It will be terrible Mrs Ryan,' he warned her. 'Dirt and noise and all sorts of horrors.'

Mr O'Brien was a man who found fault with everything, Nan Ryan told herself. She would not get upset. And in many ways it was nice to think that the house next door, which had been empty for two years since the Whites had disappeared, would soon be a home again.

She wondered who would come to live there. A family maybe. She might even baby-sit for them. She would tell the children stories and sit minding the house until the parents got back.

Her daughter Jo laughed at the very idea of a family coming to live in such a small house.

'Mam, there isn't room to swing a cat in it,' she said in her very definite, brisk way. When Jo spoke she did so with great confidence. *She* knew what was right.

'I don't know.' Nan was daring to disagree. 'It's got a nice safe garden at the back.'

'Yes, six foot long and six foot wide,' Jo said with a laugh.

Nan said nothing. She didn't mention the fact that the house in which she had reared three children was exactly the same size.

Jo knew everything. How to run a business. How to dress in great style. How to run her elegant home. How to keep her handsome husband Jerry from wandering away.

Jo must be right about the house next door. Too small for a family. Perhaps a nice woman of her own age might come. Someone who could be a friend. Or a young couple who both went out to work. Nan might take in parcels for them or let in a man to read the meter?

Bobby, who was Nan's son, said that she had better pray it wouldn't be a young couple. They'd be having parties every night, driving her mad. She would become deaf, Bobby warned. Deaf as a post. Young couples who had spent a lot doing up their house would be terrible. They would have no money. They would want some fun. They would make their own beer and ask noisy friends around to drink it with them.

And Pat, the youngest, was gloomiest of all.

'Mam will be deaf already by the time they arrive, whoever they are. Deaf from all the building noise. The main thing is to make sure they keep the garden fence the height it is and in good shape. Good fences make good neighbours they say.'

Pat worked for a security firm and felt very strongly about these things. Jo and Bobby and Pat were so very sure of themselves. Nan wondered how they had become so confident. They didn't get it from her. She had always been shy. Timid even.

She didn't go out to work because it

was the way everyone wanted it. They needed Nan at home. Their father had been quiet also. Quiet and loving. Very loving. Loving to Nan for a while, and then loving to a lot of other ladies.

One evening long ago, on her 35th birthday, Nan could take it no longer. She sat in the kitchen and waited until he came home. It was four in the morning.

'You must make your choice,' she told him.

He didn't even answer, just went upstairs and packed two suitcases. She changed the locks on the doors. It wasn't necessary. She never saw him again. He went without any speeches. Nan heard from a solicitor that the house had been put in her name. That was all she got and she didn't ask for any more since she knew it would be in vain.

She was a practical woman. She had

a small terraced house and no income. She had three children, the eldest thirteen, the youngest ten. She went out and got a job fast.

She worked in a supermarket and even took extra hours as an office cleaner to get the children through school and on their way to earning their own living. Nan had worked for nearly twenty years when the doctors said she had a weak heart and must take a great deal more rest.

She thought it was odd that they said her heart was weak. She thought it must be a very strong heart indeed to get over the fact that the husband she loved had walked out on her. She never loved anyone else.

There hadn't been time, what with working hard to put good meals in front of the children. Not to mention paying for extra classes and better clothes. There had been no family holidays over the years. Sometimes Jo, Bobby and Pat went to see their father on the train. They never said much about the visits. And Nan never asked them any questions.

Jo often brought her jackets or sweaters that she was finished with. Or unwanted Christmas presents. Bobby brought round his washing every week because he lived with Kay, this feminist girl, who said that men should look after their own clothes. Bobby often brought a cake or a packet of biscuits. He would eat these with his mother as she ironed his shirts for him. Pat came round often to fix door and window locks, or to re-set the burglar alarm. Mainly to warn her mother of all the evil there was in the world.

Nan Ryan had little to complain about. She never told her children that since she had given up work she often felt lonely. Nan's family seemed so gloomy about the work that would be done on the house next door that she didn't want to tell them that she was quite looking forward to it. That she was waiting for the builders and looking out for them every day.

Chapter Two

The builders came on a sunny morning. Nan watched them from behind her curtain. Three men altogether in a red van. The van had 'Derek Doyle' on it in big white letters.

The two younger men let themselves into Number Twelve with a key. Nan heard them call out, 'Derek! The bad news is that we'll be a week getting rid of all the rubbish that's here. The good news is that there's somewhere to plug in a kettle and it hasn't been turned off.'

A big smiling man came out of the red van.

'Well we're made for life then, for the next couple of months anyway. Isn't this a lovely road?'

He looked around at the houses and Nan felt a surge of pride. She had always thought that Chestnut Road was a fine place. Nan wished that her children had been there to see this man admiring it all. And he was a builder, a man who knew about roads and houses.

Jo used to say it was poky. Bobby said it was old-fashioned. Pat said the place was an open invitation to burglars with its long low garden walls where they could make their escape. But this man who had never seen it before liked it.

Nan hid herself and watched.

She didn't want to go out and be

there on top of them from the very start.

She saw fussy Mr O'Brien from Number Twenty-eight coming along to inspect their arrival.

'Time something was done,' he said, peering inside, dying to be invited in.

Derek Doyle was firm with him.

'Better not to let you in, sir. Don't want anything to fall on you.'

Nan's children had told her not to get too involved. Jo had said that the new owners wouldn't thank her for wasting the builders' time. Bobby had said that his girlfriend Kay said that builders preyed on women, getting them to make tea. Pat said that a house next to a building site was fair game for burglars and that she must be very watchful and spend no time talking to the men next door.

But the real reason Nan stayed out

of their way was that she didn't want to appear pushy. They would be working beside her for weeks. She didn't want them to think she was nosey. She decided she would wait until they had been there for a few days before she introduced herself. She might even keep a diary of their progress. The new owners might like it as a record of how the house had been done up for them.

Nan moved away from the front window and back to her kitchen. She ironed all Bobby's shirts. She wondered if Kay knew that Bobby brought his laundry bag over to his mother every week. But they seemed to be very happy together, so what was she worrying about?

She cleaned the silver that Jo had dropped in that morning, taking a toothbrush to get at the hard-to-reach places, like handles and legs of little jugs. She wondered why Jo worked so hard trying to impress people. But then of course it had worked, hadn't it? Jerry, who had a very wandering eye, was still with her.

Nan made a big casserole and put some of it in foil containers for the freezer. Pat worked so hard in the security firm. She worried so much, she rarely had time to shop, so she cooked very little. It was good to be able to hand her a ready-made dinner sometimes. Nan wished that Pat would take time off, dress up, go out and meet people, find a fellow.

But then what did Nan know about finding fellows or keeping them? Hers had disappeared without a word in the middle of the night twenty years ago.

Nan kept quiet on a lot of subjects. So quiet that people didn't expect her to have views any more.

There was a loud knock on the door and there stood the builder.

'Mr Doyle,' Nan said with a smile. 'You're welcome to Chestnut Road.'

He was pleased that she knew his name and seemed so friendly, and hoped that he wasn't disturbing her. But he had a problem. The instructions had been to throw out everything that he found in Number Twelve, and yet a lot of it must be of sentimental value. He wondered if perhaps as a neighbour she might know any relative or friends of the people who had once lived there. It seemed a pity to throw such things away.

'I'm Nan Ryan, come on in,' she said. They sat in the kitchen while she told him about the Whites. They were a very, very quiet couple, who hardly spoke to anyone. Mr White had a job somewhere that involved his leaving the house at six in the morning. He came back at about three with a shopping bag. His wife never left the house. They put no washing out to dry. They never invited anyone in the door. They would nod and just go about their business.

'And didn't everyone around here think they were odd?'

Derek Doyle was a kindly man, Nan thought. He cared about these people, their strange life and their private papers still in the house. It was nice to meet someone who didn't give out or complain.

Old Mr O'Brien from Number Twenty-eight would have fussed and said the Whites were selfish to have left so many problems behind them.

Her daughter Jo would have shrugged and said the Whites were nothing people. Bobby would have said that his girlfriend Kay would call Mrs White 'a professional victim'.

Pat would have said that the Whites lived like so many people, in fear of their lives from intruders.

'I didn't think they were odd. I thought they seemed content with each other,' said Nan Ryan. She thought she saw Derek Doyle look at her with admiration.

But she was being stupid. She was a woman of nearly sixty. He was a young man in his forties …

Nan told herself not to be silly.

Chapter Three

Derek Doyle dropped in every day after that. He waited until the other men had gone home, before he knocked softly on the door.

At first he used the excuse of bringing her old papers from the Whites' house. Then he just came as if he were an old friend. They called each other Nan and Derek, and indeed he was fast becoming a friend.

They didn't talk much about their families and she didn't know if he had a wife and children. Nan told him little about her son and daughters. And nothing about the husband who had left her.

He might have seen Jo, Bobby or Pat when they came in on their visits. And then again, he might not.

For a big man he was very gentle. He carried with him plastic bags belonging to Mr and Mrs White as if they were treasures. Together he and Nan went through the papers. There were lists and recipes and handy hints. There were travel brochures and medical leaflets and instruction booklets on how to work old-fashioned, out-of-date objects.

They turned them over hoping to find some understanding of a life that had ended so strangely two years ago.

'There's no mention at all of their will,' Derek said.

'No, and nothing about what he did all day at work,' replied Nan.

'If only they had kept a diary. You'd

think a woman on her own might have done that,' he said.

Nan flushed a little. She had decided to keep a diary of the building work but so far it had all been about Derek Doyle and his pleasant visits. How he had brought a rich fruitcake in a tin, and cut a slice from it for them both when he came in to tea each evening.

How she had taken the bus to the fish shop and got fresh salmon to make a sandwich for him.

How it all gave a sort of purpose to each day.

'Maybe she was afraid it might be found.'

'So she could have hidden it well,' he said with a smile.

The builders found the diary a few days later. It was behind a loose brick in the kitchen. Derek carried it in like a trophy.

'What does it say?' Nan was almost trembling.

He put down five exercise books full of small, cramped writing.

'Do you think I'd open it without you?' he asked.

She cleared a space on the table. The scones could wait. Now they might discover something about the strange secret life of the Whites, who had lived on the other side of a brick wall for twenty-five years.

They read together about the long days a woman had stayed hidden in Chestnut Road, fearful to go out lest she be discovered. Night and day she worried that the cruel husband she had left would find her and harm her again as he had done so often during their marriage.

Over and over she praised the kindness and goodness of the man she called Johnny, who must have been Mr White. How he had given up everything to save her and take her away from all the violence.

How her family thought she was dead because there had been no word from her after the night she had run away with Johnny.

'Imagine all that worry and fear right next door!' Nan's eyes were full of pity.

They ate the scones, and as they turned the pages she made them beans on toast and they had a glass of sherry.

Derek Doyle didn't leave until nearly eleven o'clock. He telephoned nobody and no one called him on his mobile.

That didn't sound like someone with a wife, Nan thought to herself. She knew it was silly but she was glad.

★

There were still two more books of the diary to read.

Several times during the day, as she heard the sound of drills and hammers, she felt tempted to go back to the table and read them. But somehow it seemed like cheating. She went out and bought lamb chops for their supper. They both felt that there might be something sad and even worrying in the final chapters.

Jo phoned.

'I might call in tonight, Mother. Jerry's got a meeting. I have to drive him there and pick him up so I could sort of kill the time with you.'

Nan frowned. This was hardly a warm thing for a daughter to say.

'I'll be out this evening,' she said.

'Oh honestly mother, tonight of all nights.' Jo was impatient, but there was nothing she could do.

Bobby rang to say he would leave his

washing in. And could she ever have it ready for him early tomorrow. Again Nan felt a wave of anger. She explained that it would not be possible.

'What will I do?' Bobby wailed.

'You'll think of something,' Nan said.

Pat rang.

'No Pat,' Nan said.

'What on earth do you mean. I haven't *said* anything yet.' Pat was annoyed.

'No to whatever you suggest,' Nan said.

'Well that's charming. I was going to go round and check your smoke alarm, but I'll save myself the journey.'

'Don't sulk Pat. I'm going out, that's all.'

'Mam, you don't *go* anywhere,' Pat protested.

Nan wondered if this was true. Was

she like poor Mrs White … who of course was not Mrs White at all. Her name was something totally different, but kind good Johnny White had gone out to work in a warehouse — a job he hated — just to keep her safe from harm.

The hours passed very slowly until it was time to take up the story again with Derek. Nan had changed into her best dress with the lace collar.

'You look very nice,' Derek said.

He had brought her a bunch of roses and she blushed as she arranged them in a vase. Then they read on.

When they got to the bit where dear Johnny had been feeling too sick to go to work but was refusing to see a doctor, Nan began to worry.

'I don't like the sound of it,' she said.

'Neither do I,' replied Derek.

They read on, about how his cancer

was terminal, how they knew she couldn't live alone without him. With tears in her eyes Nan read about the plans for the trip to the lakes, and sending their financial details and will to a solicitor.

They wanted their home at Number Twelve Chestnut Road to be sold and the proceeds given to a charity that looked after battered wives.

It had taken some time to sort it out after they had disappeared, presumed drowned in the lakes. The law moves slowly so that was why the house was empty for so long.

Nan and Derek sat as the light faded. They thought about the couple and their strange sad life.

'They must have loved each other very much,' Nan said.

'I never loved liked that,' Derek said.

'Neither did I,' said Nan.

Chapter Four

Nan told her children nothing at all about the discovery of Mrs White's diary. She was afraid that they would dismiss it, say that the Whites were boring, mad old people.

She told them nothing about Derek's visits either. Young people were so cruel. They would laugh at her and say she was being silly dressing up, and polishing things so that she could give the builder next door his tea.

But then they hadn't read the everyday thoughts of the woman who had lived a lonely frightened life until she had been rescued by her Johnny.

A woman who had continued to hide in case a man might find her. A woman who had gone out in the lakes to die with her Johnny rather than face life alone without him.

Jo, Bobby and Pat would never understand how comforting it was to sit and talk to Derek at the end of the day, and how much it had brightened up her life.

Up to now Nan had not wanted to go anywhere, meet anyone, or try anything new. In the year since she had left work she had got out of the habit of going out. She stayed in Number Fourteen waiting there in case the children called in.

Many days, of course, they did not visit but she never minded. They knew she would always be there so it was a good place for them to 'kill time', as Jo had put it the other night.

Nan hated that phrase. Why would you want to kill time? You should spend it, enjoy it, savour it.

She went to the art gallery so that she could tell Derek about the exhibition. She went to a theatre matinée. She took a bus tour around the city.

She bought three brightly coloured T-shirts in a sale and wore them one by one under her black cardigan.

'You look nice,' Derek had said when he saw the lemon or lilac or rose colours.

'You look a bit like mutton dressed as lamb Mother,' Jo had said when she saw them. 'Don't you think at your age …?'

Nan was hurt and annoyed.

'At my age I would like to be able to

do a lot of things, like buy nice clothes in a proper shop instead of buying three T-shirts for the price of two at a street stall,' she said sharply.

Jo was surprised. Mother never spoke like this.

'You're fine as you are Mother, you don't like change.' Jo tried to pat her down.

'I don't think those very loud colours suit you, Mam,' Bobby said, as he handed her his bag of laundry.

'You know where the washing machine is Bobby. Please place your dirty clothes in it and add the powder.' Nan was crisp.

'Kay was saying you need a job Mam … something to keep you busy,' Bobby said.

'I had a job for twenty years and kept you fed, clothed and educated,' Nan snapped.

Pat rang her up next morning.

'The others tell me you're becoming very ratty Mam,' she said.

'What does "ratty" mean?' Nan asked.

'I don't know really.' Pat was at a loss.

'Maybe they mean I've grown a long tail and a pointed nose, and started to scuttle around,' Nan said.

'I see what they mean, you *have* become ratty,' Pat said.

★

Derek said that there was a new Chinese restaurant at the far end of Chestnut Road. Perhaps they should try it.

Nan thought that was great. They talked about the Whites and whether Johnny had any family who knew what he had done. They debated what Mrs

White's name might have been. Nan thought it was Victoria. Derek thought it was Maud.

When he walked her home there were three notes on the door mat.

'Oh, the family must have called,' she said casually.

She saw what she thought was a look of admiration in his eyes.

'Good to have family,' Derek said.

'Yes indeed, family and friends, both very important,' Nan said.

When he had left she read the notes.

'Mam, where *are* you? Kay and I called to take you for a pint, love Bobby.'

'Mother, I have decided to treat you to a good haircut and a smart lunch out. Phone me to fix a day, Jo.'

'Mam, I could upgrade your alarm for you, getting staff discount — Jo and Bobby told me you were going on about money. We always thought Dad gave you plenty. Sorry. Love Pat.'

Nan smiled. She had really enjoyed her evening out with Derek. Now she had come home and found that at long last her children were thinking of her as a person, not just someone there to help in their lives.

Things hadn't been as good for a long time.

Chapter Five

The weeks went by and the building next door seemed to be moving along at a great rate. This didn't please Nan at all. Soon Number Twelve would be sold to strangers and the builders would go away.

She did not want to think about that day. A day when she would no longer hear Derek Doyle whistling happily with Mike and Shay next door. Evenings when there would be no tap on her door after work was finished, no hours shared.

There would be no more Sunday afternoons when she and Derek would go to see old black and white movies that they both enjoyed. It would leave a great hole in her life.

But nothing had been said. Nothing more than the fact that she was a neighbour at the job where he was now working. In a few short weeks he might be working on the other side of the city. Some other neighbour would be pouring tea for Derek Doyle.

But Nan wouldn't allow herself to be brought down. She had always looked on the best side of life.

'I wonder who the house was left to. Did they give you any idea?' she asked Derek one evening as they sat together doing a jigsaw.

He had brought it as a gift because he said he used to love them when he was a young lad but hadn't tried one for years. Derek found a complicated piece and put it in with a great flourish.

'I've no idea who it's for, I don't

think any-one knows. Ronnie the Rat, that's the developer, told us to do it up well and sell it at a high price. That's what we are doing. His orders.'

'And who ordered him?'

'The solicitor, I suppose. The one that Johnny White and his lady sent the instructions to before they went off and … before they went and did what they did …'

'I know, I know,' she said, soothing him down.

'It still upsets me,' Derek said.

'That's because you're a human being, and a good one,' Nan said.

There was a silence. It was the first time that either of them had said anything about admiring the other.

Sometimes Derek had said that she looked well. Sometimes Nan had said he was wearing a smart tie. But this was a step further.

She tried to think of something to break the silence, which hung there between them. Suddenly she found it.

'You could ask the developer who the lawyer is,' she spoke quickly.

'What do you mean?' Derek didn't understand.

'Then we'd know who the house was left to, and we might learn something about them,' Nan begged.

'But a lawyer couldn't tell, I mean it would be bound to be a secret, wouldn't it?' Derek was confused.

'Yes, you're right.' Nan hadn't thought of that.

But at least it had got her away from the dangerous ground where she had been admitting openly that she admired Derek. This was a safer area.

'Of course Ronnie the Rat might know a bit of the background himself.'

'Why do you call him that?' Nan laughed.

'He's very crooked, Ronnie is. I have to fight to make sure that the tax and VAT is paid on every job I do for him. Likes to take short cuts, our friend Ronnie Flynn.'

'Who? Who did you say?'

'Ronnie Flynn, you must have heard of him. He has a finger in every pie,' Derek said.

Nan had heard of him only too often. From her daughter Jo.

Nan usually heard of him when she was polishing silver, or ironing place mats so that Jo could impress her husband's boss, Ronnie Flynn, when he came to visit. But it was too soon to talk about such things with Derek.

'Do you think it will all be above board next door?' Nan asked.

'How do you mean?'

'I mean it would be terrible if those two people died thinking they were raising money for frightened battered women, and the money somehow didn't get to the right place …'

'No, no worries, Ronnie may be crooked, but the solicitor isn't likely to be … That house will raise plenty of money. Never fear.'

'Is Ronnie Flynn known to be crooked. I mean does everyone know this?'

'Not everyone, only people who have business deals with him. A lot of people think he's a pillar of the community.'

'I see.'

Nan did see.

Jo always spoke in such awed tones about Ronnie Flynn and his wife, and the money they raised for this charity and that. And the people they knew, and the celebrities who went to their home.

'Ronnie drops in once in a while to

see how we're getting on. I can ask him then.'

'When will he be there next?' Nan asked.

'Ah Ronnie the Rat never tells you. He trusts no one, he likes to surprise them. You get the feeling he's disappointed not to catch you out in something. Now listen to me Nan Ryan, you're neglecting your part of the jigsaw. There's loads of blue sky you haven't touched over on your side.'

She lowered her head to study the pieces.

'Will we finish this puzzle before you complete Number Twelve, do you think?' she asked in a low voice.

'Never ask a builder when anything will be finished,' Derek answered.

★

Next day Ronnie Flynn called in his

smart car to spy on the work that was taking place in Number Twelve.

He told Derek that he just happened to be in the neighbourhood. Nan watched from behind the curtain.

'You know people around here?' Derek asked.

'No, but the place is really going up. Ask round in case any of the old biddies here don't know the value of their houses and might sell cheap.'

'I'd never do that Mr Flynn,' said Derek.

'No, I suppose you wouldn't.' Ronnie the Rat shook his head.

'Have they any buyers yet for this place?' Derek asked.

'What do you mean, *they*?' Ronnie asked.

'Didn't you tell me it was owned by a firm of solicitors?' Derek looked innocent.

'Yeah, but I bought it off them. A quick sale. Got it for a song. It's up to me to sell it now.'

'I see.'

'Yeah, I think it would be a nice place to house a fancy woman,' Ronnie said with a laugh.

'Really.' Derek was cold.

'Not for me, no, no, that's not my scene. Family man me. But a couple of guys I know, they'd kill for a place to set up a bird in. Nice quiet street, no questions asked.'

Derek ended the conversation and Nan moved away from the curtain.

How terrible to think that her eldest daughter was married to someone who worked for this man.

Chapter Six

Jo called in the next morning.

She had a jacket for her mother. As a gift.

'This is much too smart for me, Jo. I don't go anywhere that I could show it off,' Nan said.

'But it would look lovely on you … it's hardly worn. Go on Mother, we can't have you wearing things off street stalls. Anyway the Flynns have seen it too often.'

'Jerry's Mr Flynn is doing up the house next door,' Nan said before she could stop herself.

'No, he can't be.' Jo was positive.

'I'm sure I saw him yesterday talking to Mr Doyle the builder.' Nan held her ground.

'No Mother, Ronnie Flynn does big apartment blocks, insurance offices, that sort of thing. Not somewhere like Chestnut Road. Believe me,' Jo said shaking her head.

'Oh well, I must have got it wrong,' Nan said. It was simpler to leave it like that.

'Anyway, I thought it was that Mr Doyle with the awful red van who was doing it up for a client.'

'No, he just got the job from a developer. He wouldn't have the money to buy a house.'

'Oh Mother, builders have a rake of money stacked away. And after all, it's only Chestnut Road, it's not as if it would cost serious money or anything.'

She looked at her mother's face.

'Sorry Mother, but you know what I mean.'

Nan said nothing.

'Now I've upset you. I didn't mean it, honestly. And this road is coming up a lot.'

'That's what the man I thought was Ronnie Flynn said,' Nan said.

Jo was relieved. 'Well now see what I mean. And enjoy the jacket, Mother, it looks lovely on you.'

With that, she was gone.

That night Nan wore the jacket when Derek Doyle came in. He looked a little startled.

'Don't you like it?' she asked.

'It's beautiful, it's just that I thought … maybe … you were going out when you were so dressed up.'

'No, I dressed up because *you* were coming to supper,' she said.

Derek smiled a big slow smile and he took one of her hands in both of his.

'Nobody ever dressed up like that for me before, not in over fifty years.'

Nan was pleased. Very pleased that he said he was over fifty. She thought the age gap might be much bigger.

Don't be silly Nan, she told herself, over and over.

★

Pat came to lunch and for the first time ever brought something to eat.

'I got you an apple tart, Mam. You're always making things for me to take home. You could have it at one of your suppers.'

'That's very good of you. But what exactly do you mean one of my suppers?'

Nan was afraid that her children would discover she saw so much of

Derek Doyle. They would laugh at her. Tell her what she knew already. That she was being silly.

'Well you must eat a big supper, you eat nothing at lunch-time,' Pat said.

Nan breathed easily again.

'Yes of course … well I'm on my own you see,' she began.

'And if you're wise that's the way you'll stay Mam,' Pat said very firmly.

'What are you saying?'

'Well *I'm* not going to get tied up with any fellow, I can tell you that for nothing!'

'But why?'

'They're no good, Mam. Look at what Dad did to you. Look at Bobby and how he won't marry Kay. Look at the way Jerry's behaving with Jo. Tell me one marriage that works. Just one would do.'

Nan was so shocked she could hardly speak.

Pat had never mentioned her father, none of them ever did. It was a subject they didn't talk about.

And what did she mean Bobby wouldn't marry Kay? Surely she understood that Kay was such a feminist that she didn't believe in marriage. And surely Jo and Jerry had a wonderful marriage. So Jo said, all the time.

Pat felt that she had won.

'There you are! You can't name one happy marriage.'

'The Whites next door, they loved each other right up to the very end.'

'Oh Mam, they were weirdos, you know nothing about them.'

'I know a lot about them,' Nan cried.

'Well then you're the only one who does. But you must admit, marriage is hopeless and it's the wise woman like yourself and myself would stay well clear of it.'

'Tell me about Jerry and Jo,' Nan said sadly.

She became even sadder as she listened.

Jerry had loads of other woman, everyone knew about it. Yes of course Jo knew, she just didn't admit it.

But now there was one serious one. Jerry might be moving out. Half of Dublin was talking about it. Jerry had a very high profile now that he was Ronnie Flynn's accountant.

'Ronnie the Rat,' Nan said to herself thoughtfully.

'What's that?'

'Nothing. And does Kay really want to get married?'

'Of course she does Mam. She says Bobby's too independent. He does his own washing, and likes to think they're just flat sharing, not actually living together.'

'And do you say any of these things to your father when you visit him?' Nan asked.

This was another first. She had never asked the children anything about their outings to the man who had left her twenty years ago.

'What visits, Mam? He has no time for us, just a series of young ones and then if they get serious he tells them you won't give him a divorce. Is that true?'

'Of course it's not.'

'Is this upsetting you, Mam?'

'Only about Jo and Bobby.'

'Well there's nothing you can do Mam. Nothing anyone can do. It's just the way things are … the way men are.'

She wanted to tell Pat that was not the way all men were, not Johnny White next door, not Derek Doyle … but she couldn't.

'There's always something we can do.'

'Don't go interfering now Mam,' warned Pat. 'You don't want to go and put your foot in it.'

'No, I'll step very carefully,' Nan said. 'Very carefully indeed.'

Chapter Seven

'I didn't mention to you that my daughter is married to a man who works as an accountant for Ronnie the Rat,' Nan said.

'Jerry, is it?' Derek asked.

'You know him?' Nan asked.

She realised that her days of keeping Derek a secret were nearly over anyway. The house next door would be finished in a couple of weeks. He would soon be gone from her life.

'I don't really *know* him,' Derek said. 'But I've met him a few times. Sharp lad he seems.'

Nan nodded. 'That's just what he is, a sharp lad. Going places, as they say.'

'He'd want to watch out that one of the places he's going isn't jail,' said Derek.

She felt as if she had swallowed a lump of ice.

'As bad as that?'

'I hate telling you this since it's family, but they're sailing very close to the wind, he and Ronnie. Money coming from all kinds of odd bank accounts, none of them from around here. Different names on company notepaper. In fact ...' Derek trailed off.

'In fact what, Derek?' Her voice was calm.

'In fact, several times I said to the lads, Mike and Shay, that I was sorry we ever took this job from Ronnie. But you see we all needed the money. Mike has a handicapped son. Shay's saving to get married. And I, well I wanted to keep the show on the road.'

'So you're sorry you took it on?' Nan hoped her voice didn't sound to disappointed.

'No, I've never worked in a place I liked more, and then there were these nice evenings to look forward to. If I'd said no to Ronnie the Rat I'd never have known all this ...' He waved his hand around her warm cosy room.

That was a lot better. Nan began to feel able to talk to him.

She was about to ask him just how deeply her son-in-law was involved when he said, 'My Rosie said that I often fall on my feet when I take on a job, but never as much as this one.'

Suddenly Nan had the cold ice feeling again.

'Rosie?' Her voice was small and thin.

'My wife,' he said.

She could hear the ticking of the clock, she could hear the traffic outside on Chestnut Road.

He had a wife.

After all these evenings, meals, outings to the cinema, it turned out that he had a wife.

She fixed a polite smile on to her face.

'Oh yes.' She knew her voice sounded shaky. *Please* may I not look too pathetic, she prayed. Please let him not see how bitterly disappointed I am.

'Well I fell on my feet too, nice company, jigsaws, films and … and everything. I enjoyed it all very much too, I must say. You could tell Rosie that from me.'

He looked at her confused. 'I won't be telling Rosie anything about all this.'

'Suit yourself.' She was clipped now. Cold.

'You don't tell *your* family about my visits here,' he said.

'No, well, that's a bit different,' Nan said.

'I don't see why,' he began.

'Derek, could you please tell me what you think that I should know about Jerry and his being involved in something that's against the law.'

'No, why should I gossip? That's what's so great about you and me … we don't rejoice in gossip like the rest of the world … telling little bits of information, telling tales.'

She looked at him with new eyes.

Yes, she had liked that about Derek Doyle. He kept his business to himself.

But she hadn't realised that he had kept to himself the fact that he was married. Some marriage it must be, with Derek going back to the bosom of the family after eleven every night. Not to mention being away at the cinema on weekends. Did he tell this to the patient, understanding Rosie, whoever she was?

Nan felt that Rosie deserved all she got. Imagine telling a husband that he fell on his feet when he found another conquest. She spoke calmly.

'I agree, and I *don't* usually gossip. I never interfere, but this is a time when I may need to do both. I heard today that Jerry was having an affair with another woman.'

'Yes I know,' said Derek. '*And* she's pregnant.'

'I don't believe you!'

'I'm sorry to break it to you like this, but Ronnie had said that he thought next door would be ideal for Jerry's girlfriend to live in. He said that Jerry had refused even to consider it.'

'Yes, he'd hardly want her living next door to his mother-in-law.' Nan's face was hard.

'Does your daughter know all about it?' His voice was gentle and very kind.

'I don't really know,' Nan said.

'It's not fair, lovely girl like that. He shouldn't be playing around on her.'

'You know her?' Nan was surprised.

'I see the three of them coming in and out to visit you during the day. Jo is the blonde one with the smart car.'

Imagine he had been interested enough to notice them all. But that didn't matter now.

'She'll get over it. People do.'

Derek shook his head. 'Men like that are just selfish. Jerry will be caught out in the end. I know money isn't everything, but for her sake I hope your girl gets out while he still has some assets.'

'As you say, money isn't everything,' Nan said. Her tone was very cold.

Derek leaned across the table.

'Have I said something to upset you Nan? Perhaps I should have kept my mouth closed about Ronnie's accountant.'

'No, not at all.' Nan was still very distant. 'No, indeed I would have had to know sometime.'

That evening she offered no dessert even though he could see there was half an apple tart in the kitchen with a jug of cream.

Derek Doyle left Nan Ryan's house at nine o'clock.

Earlier than he had for a long time.

Chapter Eight

'Bobby?'

'Yes Mam, is anything wrong?' Nan didn't usually call her son. And never at nine-thirty in the evening.

'No, nothing at all. Just, can you call in to me on your way home from work tomorrow. I'd like that.'

'Something *is* wrong.'

'No, I told you. And Bobby, don't bring your laundry. Never bring it again. Learn to use your own washing machine and ask Kay if she'll teach you how to iron.'

'I don't think …'

'Well I do. And offer to iron her blouses and shirts too … she can't say you're anti-feminist then, can she?'

She hung up and called Pat.

'I'm not sure Mam, I have a lot to do.'

'You have nothing to do, Pat. That's what's wrong with you. You spend hours fearing imaginary burglars …'

'They are *not* imaginary Mam!'

'Most of yours are. You live in a flat that hasn't been cleaned or tidied. You couldn't invite anyone back there — a burglar wouldn't even stay! You haven't combed your hair in weeks. Get your hair cut at lunch-time and try to look presentable tomorrow evening.'

'I have to suppose that you're drunk Mam,' said Pat in amazement. 'I've never heard you talk like this.'

Then she called Jo. Jo answered the phone on the first ring.

'Oh Mother,' she said, disappointed. 'I thought it was Jerry.'

'No it's only your mother.' Nan spoke briskly. 'I'd like you to come to have lunch with me here tomorrow …'

'Mother, I'm not sure that's possible … You see I don't really eat big lunches in people's houses …'

'I'll be having a tuna and tomato salad, you can eat whatever you like. I need to talk to you, Jo. I'd be glad if you could be here about one o'clock.'

Well, they're all coming, she thought to herself as she prepared for bed. Was it really as easy as this to be firm and refuse to take no for an answer?

Should she perhaps have done it long ago?

It didn't matter. She was doing it now.

Next morning Nan looked across from the kitchen window at Number

Twelve. There was no singing and whistling from Derek Doyle today. Nan wondered whether Rosie had packed him sandwiches. Whether he had kissed her goodbye.

She wondered too about the woman she called Mrs White, who had hidden in that house for so long, trembling until her Johnny came home and she felt safe again.

Had she been a fool to live like that with him, and to die with him?

Should she not have gone to the courts and got legal protection from the bully she married?

Should Nan herself have been much more tough twenty years ago, when her husband had walked out? Should she have demanded that he give her proper support to bring up the children, instead of working herself to the bone to earn the money?

Or should she have played it differently ... talked it all over with him, reasoned, asked him to explain why he preferred the other woman to her?

After all he hadn't stayed with her long. It couldn't have been a *real* romance? It was too late to change any of these things now.

She hoped she would have the strength to get through today and all she had planned to achieve. She opened her front door when she knew the men would be there.

'See you this evening around seven then Derek?' she called out to the builder.

He looked surprised. They had never acknowledged in front of Mike and Shay that he had been calling. He was startled.

'Sure, yes, that would be ... em ... grand Mrs ... em ... Ryan.'

Then she got everything ready, both on the table and in her mind, for lunch with her daughter.

'I hope this is important Mother,' Jo said when she arrived. 'After all, we could talk any old time couldn't we?'

'I hope I don't make a mess of this Jo,' Nan said. And Jo saw tears in her mother's eyes.

'Come on Mother, out with it,' she said.

It turned out that Jo had known about everything except the pregnancy. And that annoyed her more than she could say.

Jerry had always said he wasn't ready for children. Well now, imagine that! It turned out that he had been only too ready. She even laughed at the thought that Ronnie was offering Jerry the house in Chestnut Road to solve his problems.

'You've made up my mind for me, Mother … you have. Just by telling me this. I've been dithering for ages but now I know what I am going to do. I'm leaving him.'

'But don't you love him?' Nan asked.

'No, not for a long time.'

'So why didn't you leave before?'

'I thought if I ignored it, it would go away. After all, I have much more to offer than she has … the other one.' Jo looked sad for a moment.

'I know Jo, but you know how men are always looking for something new. I went through the same with your father.'

'No, he admires me. I used to think that was important. You see he's impressed that I have my own business, and that I made him invest any clean money he had in that. When he and Ronnie and the pregnant girlfriend all go under, I won't be any part of the fall.'

She looked hard but in control.

'Thank you, Mam, you've done me a real favour. Thank you for having the courage.'

Nan was speechless.

'Is there anything I can do for you, Mam? Please.'

'Yes, there is,' Nan said slowly. 'Could you come to supper this evening around seven o'clock? The others are coming and I want you to meet a friend of mine.'

'What friend, Mother?'

'Around seven tonight,' Nan said.

Chapter Nine

Nan was ready in plenty of time. She dressed carefully. After all, she had practically ordered her daughter Pat to smarten herself up.

Jo always looked like a fashion model. Nan didn't want to look old and shabby compared to them. She had a bottle of sherry and five glasses on a tray. And a chicken casserole in the oven.

Number Fourteen Chestnut Road wasn't used to this kind of entertaining. Since Nan's husband had disappeared all that time ago any spare money went towards buying shoes and schoolbooks.

She wondered which of them would arrive first. In fact she was quite excited.

Bobby came first.

'What did you want me for, Mam?'

'Dear dear dear … that's not very nice Bobby. I ask my only son to supper and this is the response. I wanted to see you and give you a nice meal. What else?'

'But you never want me here Mam, except to do my washing,' he said, confused.

'Don't be idiotic, Bobby! Seriously, you sound like a half-wit. Do you think I *liked* doing your laundry?'

'All right Mam, I did my washing last night and actually Kay seemed pleased. She said it made the place seem more like a real home.'

'Good.'

'But why exactly …?'

Just then Derek knocked on the door. He was carrying a potted violet. He was startled to find Bobby there, and made a move as if to leave again.

'Come in Derek, nice to see you. This is my son Bobby. Bobby, Derek Doyle is in charge of the building work next door.'

Both men looked baffled but before they could do more than shake hands Pat had arrived. Bobby looked at her amazed.

'What have you done to yourself? You look completely different,' he said.

'Pat just dressed up for supper with her mother as any grateful person would do.'

Nan looked with approval at Pat's shining well-cut hair. And she wore a brand new red jacket over a navy skirt.

Normally she wouldn't be seen in anything except jeans and a big sweater.

'My daughter Pat,' Nan said proudly.

'And very nice you look too,' Derek said politely. 'I've seen you coming in and out to visit your mother. You look charming tonight.'

Pat shuffled and smiled with pleasure.

'Delighted to meet you, Mr Doyle,' she said.

They were busy talking about security on building sites when Jo arrived. Her face was pale but she was calm.

'The deed is done Mother,' she said quickly on the doorstep.

'You weren't too hasty, I hope,' Nan said.

'There are times when you *know*

you are doing the right thing. Then it's better to do it swiftly.'

'I know exactly what you mean,' said Nan.

And she did. She knew that tonight's little gathering was saving her dignity. She was not going to be made a fool of. Not by anyone and certainly not someone she had liked and admired as much as Derek.

'The others are here?' Jo was surprised when she heard the voices of her brother and sister.

'Yes, indeed. I've made us all supper and now you'll have a glass of sherry.' Nan led her daughter into the room and over to the tray of little glasses as if this was a normal happening in Number Fourteen Chestnut Road.

Jo's mouth dropped when she saw Pat.

'Did you have a makeover or what?' she gasped.

'I bought a new jacket, yes,' Pat said crossly.

'This is Derek Doyle who runs the building next door,' Nan began.

'Mr Doyle, how nice to meet you.' Jo had an easy, practised way of talking to people that always made them smile.

'My mother says you are making a wonderful job of Number Twelve. Fit for anyone, a princess even!'

Jo's eyes were too bright. She was very over-excited.

Derek seemed to realise this. He was good at calming people.

Nan thought with a pang about how well Derek had managed old bores like fussy Mr O'Brien from Number Twenty-eight. She remembered how he had soothed the neighbours who complained about the builders' skip outside the door, and offered to take their household rubbish for them.

Here he was making sure that Jo didn't build up to some kind of a tantrum.

'It's easy to make a good job of a house in *this* street. They were very well built originally, good thick walls. The rooms have nice proportions ...' He looked admiringly around the sitting room they were in.

'And what kind of people might buy it, do you think? I'm only interested since I'd like to know what kind of neighbours my mother will have.'

Derek seemed to hear the touch of hysteria in her voice. He was calmer than ever.

'Well it depends on who Mr Flynn will sell it to. He bought the house at a very low price, but of course he's a businessman and so he is hoping to make a good profit on it.'

Jo gave a snort. 'You bet he is!'

'But perhaps your husband as his accountant —'

'My ex-husband.' Jo interrupted.

Nan was relieved that nobody dropped a sherry glass.

'You're not serious?' Pat gasped.

'Since when?' asked Bobby.

'Would you all like to sit down at the table?' Nan's tone was bright. 'We don't want the chicken to get cold.'

Now they all looked with astonishment at Nan.

They moved to obey her, wordless, amazed that she was taking such huge news so very calmly.

'This is all very nice.' Derek began to break the silence. 'Smells just great.'

'You're great, Mother,' Jo agreed.

'Well I wanted you all to meet each other. Derek has been coming in a lot after work so I wanted him to meet my family …'

They all looked from one to the other as if it were a tennis match. They realised that there was some great tension here, but they didn't know what it was.

'Yes indeed, and a delightful family it is,' Derek said, struggling desperately.

'*And* of course I wanted you to meet him.' Nan smiled round at them all from the top of the table.

'Unfortunately, Derek's wife Rosie hasn't been able to come with him tonight. She would have been very welcome. You must bring Rosie over here sometime Derek, before you finish Number Twelve. You will, won't you?'

As she started to ladle out the

chicken casserole onto the plates, Nan did not see how Derek's face had crumpled up, as if somebody had hit him a very heavy blow.

Chapter Ten

Afterwards they wondered what would have happened that night if all the other people had not arrived.

First to knock on the door was Kay, Bobby's girlfriend.

'I just happened to be passing by, Mrs Ryan, and I knew Bobby had been invited to supper here … so I … well I …' Her voice trailed away.

'Come in and join us, Kay. Bobby should have asked you in the first place.'

'You didn't say to ask her, I thought

it was just family!' Bobby did not want to be blamed.

'But Kay is family in every sense, isn't she?' Nan was bright and casual as she introduced Derek and got another plate for Kay.

'You look so different, Pat,' Kay remarked suddenly. 'Like a new person altogether.'

'Thank you Kay,' Pat said.

She was even behaving differently. Nan realised that the old Pat would have shrugged and been unable to accept the praise.

Nan and Kay seemed the only people able to have a conversation. The other four were struck with a strange silence. It was as if they had heard too much news already and there was no place for idle chat.

'Oh Jo, your husband came round to

our flat looking for Bobby. He seemed upset.'

'He's not my husband,' Jo said. 'He's my ex-husband, and I hope he's very upset.'

'Heavens,' said Kay.

It seemed such a mild thing to say under the circumstances but she couldn't think of anything else.

'Did you know this, Bobby?' she asked.

'I know nothing. Nothing about anything,' Bobby said, very firmly.

'*I'm* sorry Jo,' Kay said politely.

'Well I'm not, and I'm the one who was married to him. If it hadn't been for Mother's friend Mr Doyle here I might never have known how far he'd gone.'

'Oh dear, I didn't mean to be putting my big foot in it,' Derek began.

'You didn't, you just made things clear,' Jo assured him.

'No, it was none of my business. I should have kept my mouth closed,' Derek said. 'It's done nothing but harm, my interfering. If I could have the last twenty-four hours over again I would, believe me.'

'But why? You only said what was true, Mr Doyle. Better that I should know sooner than later.'

There was another knock on the door.

'I'll go,' Bobby said.

They could hear him on the doorstep, saying 'Who will I say wants her?' With that, a man pushed past him and entered the room.

It was Ronnie Flynn, the developer.

'Sorry to bother you, Mrs Ryan, but I've just had my accountant on to me moaning that I told you all his private business. I wanted you to confirm that I never told you a single word …' He stopped when he saw Jo.

'Oh hello Jo, I didn't see you.'

'No Ronnie, I can see you didn't.'

'It's just that it's a bit of a mess.'

'Indeed it is Ronnie. A great mess, but let's not worry everyone with the details.' Jo's smile was bright and insincere.

Ronnie looked around further and saw Derek Doyle.

'God almighty, Derek, what on earth are you doing here?'

'I was asked to supper here Ronnie. Mrs Ryan kindly invited me to meet her family.' Derek seemed at ease.

'Family? You're part of the family that lives here Jo? Here on Chestnut Road?'

'Yes indeed Ronnie, this is my mother's house, my mother's supper party that you've suddenly barged in to …'

'And of course if you'd like to join us.' Nan Ryan was quite unflappable tonight.

'No, Mother, I'm sure Ronnie has to get on home, or did you want to talk about Number Twelve with Mr Doyle?'

'All this can be sorted out you know, Jo, there's no need to make such a production out of it.'

'Oh I do agree with you,' Jo smiled a very cold smile. 'That's just what I said to Jerry this afternoon before going to my lawyer. No need for a song and dance, I said. No need for the details of everything to come out if he's reasonable.'

'The details?' Ronnie's voice was a whisper.

'No need on earth for all his business deals to be brought to the public eye. I mean who wants to know what he and you paid for that house at Number Twelve next door, or what you're going to sell it for?'

'And what did he say?' Ronnie and Jo seemed to be having a private conversation. It was as if they had forgotten anyone else was in the room.

'Well I think he sort of saw the sense of it. Not happy about it of course. That's why he must have come after you and — what was it you said — moaned at you?'

'I'll go now, I'm very sorry for interrupting your party, Mrs Ryan. I didn't know, you see.'

'No of course you didn't.' Nan soothed him.

'Lord, I wonder who'll come next!' Pat said when Ronnie had gone out the door.

'Second helpings anyone?' Nan asked.

'And why wasn't your wife able to come, Derek?' asked Bobby, thinking he was helping with the conversation.

'For two reasons. Because she wasn't invited and because I haven't seen her for fourteen years,' Derek replied.

'Well, and I thought we'd *had* all the surprises tonight. I was wrong,' Jo said.

'You never said.' Nan's voice was low.

'You never asked,' said Derek

'You never mentioned her at all until last night when you told me that she said you always fell on your feet, getting neighbours to cook for you when you went on building jobs.'

'So she did. She said that a long time ago, before she disappeared with one of my mates.'

Now these two were talking as if there was no one else in the room.

'I'm sorry,' Nan said.

'I was at the time, but I got over it. There were no children. I learned to build my life as I imagine you did when your husband left.'

'And how did you know?'

'Mr Johnson, Number Twenty-eight, always believes people should be informed,' Derek said, and they smiled at each other across the table.

There was a knock on the door. This time Pat went to answer it.

It was Jerry. Could he have a word with Jo?

Pat checked back at the dining table.

'Apparently not, Jerry,' she said.

'Well just tell her, everything she wants. Just no details, no business details. She'll understand.'

'I think we all understand,' Pat said, and closed the door.

And somehow they all *did* understand.

Kay and Bobby understood that they were much more committed to each other than either of them had admitted.

Jo understood that her sister Pat would be a fine companion to go out clubbing with.

And Derek Doyle and Nan Ryan understood a lot of things.

That Derek should buy Number Twelve.

And then he and Mike and Shay would build a huge arch between the two sitting rooms, so that Nan and Derek would have a really fancy house between them.

And they knew they would travel

together, and they would do jigsaw puzzles.

And they would make sure that the house where the Whites had lived in fear would become a happy home and that proper money would go to the charity so that what they had done at the lakeside was not in vain.

They didn't know all this at once.

But they knew a lot of it.